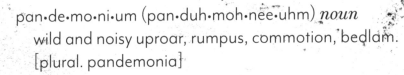

pan·de·mo·ni·um (pan·duh·moh·nee·uhm) *noun*
wild and noisy uproar, rumpus, commotion, bedlam.
[plural. pandemonia]

PAN·DA·MO·NI·A (pan·duh·moh·nee·uh) *noun informal*
complete and utter chaos, often following the disturbance
of a blissfully sleeping panda.

For Lucy and Harvey — C.O.

For all the animal lovers fighting to keep this world wonderful — C.N.

Chris Owen is a former paper boy, supermarket shelf stacker, apple picker and radio journalist. These days he's a primary school teacher living in North Perth with his wife and two young rapscallions, a couple of crazy crabs, three goldfish and numerous tadpoles.

Chris Nixon is an illustrator and creative director from Perth, Western Australia.
No animals were harmed in the process of Chris becoming an artist,
apart from the time he worked as a fishmonger.

PANDAMONIA

CHRIS OWEN AND CHRIS NIXON

Kane Miller
A DIVISION OF EDC PUBLISHING

So you're here at the zoo on this glorious day.

You're sure to have fun – it's a great place to play.

Come in. Look around. Relax and explore.

Inside you will find there are creatures galore.

You'll have a magnificent time at the zoo ...

... just don't wake the panda whatever you do.

If you wake up the panda he gets very grumpy,

which hypes up the hippos and makes them all jumpy.

When the hippos get jumpy they usually hop,

and once they begin, they are tricky to stop.

Those hippos create such a hullabaloo ...

... so don't wake the panda whatever you do.

When the hippos start hopping, the termites get tickly.

They make the echidna incredibly prickly.

For though, as you probably know, they are titchy,

cantankerous termites are awfully itchy.

They torment the toes of the elephants too ...

... so don't wake the panda whatever you do.

The zebra, giraffe and hyenas all laugh.

The geckos and gibbons all giggle.

Which causes the emus to shimmy and sway,

and the tapirs' bottoms to jiggle.

The chimps chit-chatter.

The ducks start quacking.

The jabirus jabber

and the yaks start yakking.

So waking the panda might spark off a riot,

and that's why we like to keep things nice and quiet.

When the yaks start yakking, the frogs start humming.

The bilbies bop. The baboons start drumming.

The air is filled with a deafening din,

sending the wallabies into a spin.

They bounce to the beat with the red kangaroo ...

... so don't wake the panda whatever you do.

If the wallabies bounce, the bats start swinging.

The scarlet macaws and galahs start singing.

Their swinging and singing sets off the raccoon,

whose barking is usually way out of tune.

That raucous raccoon makes a racket, it's true ...

... so don't wake the panda whatever you do.

The snakes serenade as the peacocks parade
and the devils start gnashing their jaws.
And when the koala whips up more palaver,
the penguins break into applause.

The wombats wiggle. Orangutans romp.
The lemurs leap and the rhinos stomp.
The ground vibrates and the treetops shake.
Yes, waking the panda would be a mistake.

When the treetops shake, the sloth starts to shuffle,

which ends up creating a mighty kerfuffle.

For though sloths are slow and appear rather lazy,

if they're in the mood they can really go crazy.

The crocodile, too, starts snapping on cue.

So don't wake the panda.

Don't wake the panda.

No, don't wake the panda whatever you do.

When the crocodile snaps, the lion will ROAR!

The bison and buffalo bellow for more.

A frenzy of animals flocks to the floor,

and that's when you know there is trouble in store.

The black cockatoos like to screech rock 'n' roll.

The toucans can cancan right out of control.

The grizzly bears start to rumba as well,

and even the tortoise comes out of her shell.

Flamingos and dingoes all do the fandango.

The chinchillas cha-cha.

The tamarins tango.

Yes, waking the panda could cause a stampede,

and here at the zoo

that's the last thing we need.

There's grunting and growling and prancing and prowling,
skipping and scowling and squealing and yowling,
squeaking and squawking, snarling and snorting,
hysterical howling, chaotic cavorting.

Then just when you think that the rhythm might slow,

the beasts go WILD and louder they grow.

Into the night the shenanigans flow,

as they dance in the light of the glowworms' glow, singing

ZOO-BOP-A-LOO-BOP-A

So don't wake the panda.

Please, don't wake the panda.

No, don't wake the panda whatever you do!

Oops ...